Spine Chilling

Vengeful Spirits
Book 2

Michelle Godard-Richer

Copyright © 2024 by Michelle Godard-Richer

Layout design and Copyright © 2024 by Next Chapter

Published 2024 by Next Chapter

Edited by Alicia Dean

Cover art by Lordan June Pinote

This book is a work of fiction. Names, characters, places, and incidents are the product of the author's imagination or are used fictitiously. Any resemblance to actual events, locales, or persons, living or dead, is purely coincidental.

All rights reserved. No part of this book may be reproduced or transmitted in any form or by any means, electronic or mechanical, including photocopying, recording, or by any information storage and retrieval system, without the author's permission.

Other Titles by Michelle Godard-Richer

Into The Fog

The Fatal Series:

Fatal Hunt

Fatal Witness

Fatal Stand

The Hinchcliffe Sisters:

Back in Time with Jelly Beans

Forward in Time with Jelly Beans

Vengeful Spirits:

Angel of Death

To my family

Chapter One

WITH SHAKING HANDS, Peter McFadden used what little strength he had to clutch his vintage copy of *The Turn of the Screw* to his chest. He didn't have much time left, and he prayed the incantation he'd found in an old occult tome would work. Black tendrils of death circled him the same way he'd circled his prey before his illness sidelined him.

From childhood into his teenage years, he'd fought against dark thoughts and urges to inflict harm upon others. One Friday night, after passing around a bottle of rum with his friends Jimmy and Hank in the forest behind their high school, his control had slipped. Even though he'd been tipsy, he remembered what happened as if it were yesterday and not forty years ago.

Before that night, he'd only ever snuck a sip of his father's beer from time to time. The rum that night hit him hard. He didn't like the swimmy sensation in his head, and he wanted it to go away. He stood. "Guys, I don't feel good. I'm going home to bed."

Jimmy laughed and burped at the same time. He slurred, "Look at the big baby. He wants to go home to his mommy."

Hank tipped his head back and momentum took over. He

tumbled backwards off the log he sat on and landed on his back. He joined in the laughter and clutched his stomach.

Peter clenched his fists and stomped towards the two boys who continued to laugh at his expense. Jimmy was a toxic friend. One minute he'd play nice, then the next he'd make a joke at Peter's expense. The years of humiliation compounded into this one moment in time.

He shoved Jimmy off the log, sat on his chest, then wrapped his hands around Jimmy's throat and squeezed.

Jimmy's eyes widened, and he wheezed. He grabbed at Peter's wrists, trying, but failing to pull his hands away from his throat.

A pleasant rush of adrenaline cleared some of the fuzzy sensation in Peter's head as the life slipped out of Jimmy's eyes. The struggle to hold onto control and suppress the darkness no longer chained Peter down. He felt free to be himself for the first time in his life.

Hank stopped laughing when he turned his head their way. "What are you doing, Pete? Stop! You're gonna kill him!" He teetered as he got to his feet.

"Too late. He's already dead." Peter had researched different ways to kill, and strangulation was one of the quietest and fastest—thirty seconds until unconsciousness and five minutes until brain death.

Hank stared at Jimmy's lifeless body and tears filled his eyes. He kneeled by Jimmy's head and shook his shoulders. "Wake up, man."

"He's not sleeping. He's dead." Peter stood and grinned at Hank. "And you're next."

A stain formed on the front of Hank's blue jeans, and he crawled backwards like a crab skittering away from a chef with a raised knife. He wouldn't get far. Hank and Jimmy had had a lot more rum than Peter.

Peter caught up to Hank in less than a minute and sat on his chest. His maniacal laughter echoed through the forest as he squeezed the life out of Hank. He double checked both boys for a pulse, making sure they were dead before he left the forest and snuck back into his bedroom.

No one ever knew he'd been with Jimmy and Hank that night. All three of them had snuck out of their bedroom windows, and none of their parents had known where they were. The police had come to talk to him, and his parents were adamant he'd been home in bed all night.

Forty years later, he lay in bed wasting away with all his dark, but happy memories. Stomach cancer had ravaged his body to the point where he could no longer bear to eat or drink. The weight had gradually slipped away, leaving him so thin, he hated glimpsing his own skeletal reflection.

His eyes fluttered and he sensed his life slipping away. He turned his head to stare into the beady eyes of his beloved pet crow, perched in his cage in the corner. "Goodbye, Ezekiel, my faithful friend. We'll see each other again."

Chapter Two

Esme Engelbert glanced around her dead father's cluttered bedroom and groaned. The looming task of emptying his entire house, combined with the grief of her loss, sucked every drop of her energy dry.

"Luce, he has so much stuff. This is going to take *forever*." She opened the closet. A musty version of body odor escaped the confines of the small space, and she wrinkled her nose. "Look at all those old clothes! He has four garbage bags full in here and they stink. He never got rid of anything."

Her sister Lucy shrugged. "Well, you could pay somebody to get rid of all Dad's crap. I don't think there's enough in his savings to cover more than his cremation though."

"Those junk removal services aren't cheap. I don't have the money. Do you?"

"I do. But I don't want to spend a dime on that worthless sack. He treated us and Mom like garbage. I'll never forget how sick Mom got during her chemo, and he wouldn't stop his stupid camping trips to stay home and take care of us. I was never prouder of Mom than I was when she divorced his ass."

Esme shoved down her irritation at her sister's callous behavior. "It's not right to speak ill of the dead. No one's perfect. Dad tried to be nice towards the end."

Caw!

Esme jumped and turned to face her father's pet crow perched in the giant cage standing in the corner of the room. "Sweet Jesus, that bird scared the crap out of me."

The crow met her gaze with his soulless, beady eyes. "Razzhole!"

Lucy narrowed her eyes at the bird. "Did he call you an asshole? I'll make you a deal. I'll foot the bill for the junk removal, but you have to take Ezekiel home with you."

"Ah, about that. My building doesn't allow pets. He's a predator. I bet if we let him loose outside, he'll be fine on his own. Dad used to let him loose in the woods all the time."

"Whatever. But you let him out of the cage."

"I can't believe you're making me do this. Look at those mean, beady eyes." Esme opened the bedroom window and removed the screen. She took a shuddering breath and rested her hand on the opening of the cage. "Ezekiel, you're free. Please don't attack us. Just go find mice to eat or something." Esme opened the cage, then curled into a ball on the ground with her arms covering her head.

Lucy said, "You're such a coward, Esme. It's just a pet bird."

Caw!

Big wings flapped overhead. Esme wanted to know where Ezekiel was, but she also didn't want her eyes pecked out.

"Ouch!" Lucy screamed. "You're the asshole!"

Esme lifted her head.

A line of blood trickled from Lucy's forehead onto her cheek. She swung a lamp at Ezekiel's head.

The bird dodged the lamp and flew out the window.

Lucy slammed the window shut. "Some help you are. You're such a wimp."

Esme swallowed the response that came to mind. *Or maybe I'm just smarter than you.* She grabbed a shirt off a chair and ran over to her sister. "It doesn't look bad. It's a tiny gash. You won't need stitches." She pressed the fabric against the wound. The bleeding had already slowed.

Lucy held the shirt in place. "Go find me a bandage. Then we'll see if there's anything valuable in this heap."

Esme rolled her eyes as she crossed the hall to the bathroom and rummaged through the medicine cabinet.

What a bitch!

Would it hurt Lucy to say please once in a while? She came across a box with a single bandage left in it. She opened it and positioned it on Lucy's forehead. "I bet his book collection is worth something. Some of his first editions are antique."

"Ooh, probably. And he always kept a gun under the bed. That would be worth money." Lucy crouched on the floor and lifted the comforter.

Esme kneeled beside her sister and angled the flashlight on her phone into the dark space beneath the box spring. The beam illuminated two boxes. A black metal box and a big shoe box.

Lucy pulled the boxes out. "If he had anything valuable in this room it would be inside these." She tugged the metal box towards her and lifted the latches. "Yep, this is his old Colt. We'll take this with us. What's in that one?"

With an unexplainable sense of unease lifting the hair on the back of her neck, Esme pulled the shoe box towards her and flipped it open. "This is weird." She picked up a bundle of cards, with a woman's driver's license on top, held together by an elastic band. She tugged the elastic off and spread what turned out to be a bunch of driver's licenses across the carpet. They all belonged to young women. "What the hell, Luce? Why would he have these?"

"I don't know. I'll google the names." Lucy's fingers flew across her iPhone. Her skin turned clammy, and her hands shook.

"What's wrong, Luce?"

"Ohmigod. I've searched three of the names so far, and they were all murdered by the Colorado Strangler. And the police still haven't caught him. But that still doesn't explain why Dad has these." Lucy picked up a small jewelry box, the only other thing left in the shoe box. "I wonder what's in here."

Esme's stomach twisted into a tight knot as her brain worked through the shock of their discovery and arrived at a horrific conclusion. "I wouldn't touch that if I were you."

"Why not?" Lucy opened the box, then dropped it, and covered her mouth.

The box landed on its side and a mound of gleaming white teeth spilled out all over the carpet. Almost as if their father had polished each tooth individually after...he yanked them out of someone's mouth.

Esme backed away. "Don't touch those, Luce."

"I'm not planning on it. What do we do with them?"

Esme stood, took Lucy's hand, and helped her stand on shaky legs. "We need to call the police."

"Ohmigod! Do you think Dad..."

"Considering the Colorado Strangler got his name from strangling his victims, then removing their teeth—that would explain Dad's collection. Wouldn't it? Our father was a serial killer."

Chapter Three

Two months later

ON FRIDAY THE 13ᵀᴴ, Davis Shetland stepped into The Tome Boutique, his favorite book store. He ignored the recent bestseller section and continued past the mystery and romance shelves to a display case at the back of the store near the cash register. All the older and more valuable books were kept there. He anticipated discovering a certain book he'd wanted for a long time.

The shop owner, Mr. Conway, an older gentleman with wire-rimmed glasses came around the counter. His signature olive-green tweed blazer with brown patches on the elbows hung from his skinny shoulders. "Nice to see you again, Mr. Shetland. What can I interest you in today?"

"Has anything new come in?" Davis leaned and peered inside the glass case. A few books caught his eye, in particular, what appeared to be a slightly battered first edition of *The Turn of the Screw* by Henry James. He didn't want to seem too interested, or Mr. Conway would adjust the asking price accordingly.

Mr. Conway's cheeks flushed. He cleared his throat and adjusted his tie. "Well, most of the books in the case arrived yesterday."

"What's wrong, Mr. Conway? Are you feeling ill?"

"I'm fine. It's the origin of the books. To be honest, I regret buying them. I'm only telling you because you're a regular customer."

"Yes?"

"They belonged to Peter McFadden, the suspected Colorado Strangler."

Davis took a step back, feigning discomfort. Maybe it would bring the asking price down. "Oh, that's rather morbid."

"It is. I'm hesitant to advertise the origins of this collection for fear the wrong sorts of customers will swarm my shop or try to rob me."

"I understand. I won't tell anyone. What's the asking price on *The Poems of Edgar Allan Poe* and...maybe *The Turn of the Screw*?"

"Hmmm..." Mr. Conway shifted his glasses farther up his nose. "Well, since you're a regular, I could accept $2500 for the Edgar Allan Poe. *The Turn of the Screw* is slightly battered and less popular, so $850."

"Would you settle for $800 on *The Turn of the Screw*?"

Mr. Conway smiled then pulled a key ring out of his pocket and opened the case. "It's all yours, Mr. Shetland."

Davis suppressed the urge to smile and dance around the shop. He'd wanted to get his hands on this book for years. But he needed to keep his poker face intact for future negotiations. Instead of celebrating, he handed over his credit card.

He carried his new treasure in a brown paper bag as he crossed the street and climbed inside his black Mustang. "Woohoo!" He fired up the engine, peeled away from the curb, then drove home.

Clutching the bag to his chest, Davis strode to the front door of his cozy, brown-bricked bungalow.

Caw! Razzhole!

"What in the...?" Davis spun. A crow perched in the Rocky Mountain juniper in his front yard. "Did you just call me an asshole?"

Caw! The bird stared at him with beady, malicious eyes.

"I must have misheard." Davis shook his head, unlocked the door, then stepped inside.

He hung his coat on the black metal rack inside the entrance and kicked off his dress shoes on the welcome mat. Clutching the paper bag to his chest, he beelined it to the bookshelf in his reading nook.

Davis opened the bag, shut his eyes, and focused on inhaling the delicious mixed scents of almonds and vanilla emitted by old books. Of all the books he'd collected so far, *Great Expectations, A Christmas Carol,* and *Pride and Prejudice* were his favorites. His new treasure would be a welcome addition.

With a gentle touch, he took *The Turn of the Screw* out of the bag, removed the bubble wrap, and placed it on the end of his top shelf. He stood back and admired the spines of his books. Once placed on the shelf, he never touched them again. Rather than disturbing the physical copies, he read the eBook versions instead.

A shadow shifted out of the corner of his eye, and at the same time, the crow cawed outside his window. A sense of unease settled over him. He searched the room for the source of the shadow. Nothing unusual or out of place caught his eye. He didn't have any pets and he lived alone. The only moving shadow in his house should be his own.

"I must be seeing things."

He disregarded the instinct warning him of something amiss and stuck leftover lasagna in the microwave for dinner. Eager to settle into his reading nook, he shoveled the lukewarm lasagna in his mouth as fast as he could chew and swallow.

Thankfully, it was Friday. The weekend would be a much-needed reprieve from the nightmare that was work. He regretted switching careers from developing apps to managing a tech support division. All the difficult and angry customers were redirected to him, and lately, he'd dealt with more of them than usual.

People were the worst. Books made for much better company. With his girlfriend Esme out of town, he had the whole weekend ahead of him to read in peace. He'd need to keep the origins of his latest purchase to himself. She'd refused to let him near her father's books, not wanting to encounter any reminders of him and his dark past.

He settled into the brown recliner next to his precious bookshelf, picked up his Kindle Paperwhite, and bought the eBook version of *The Turn of the Screw*. While reading, his gaze traveled from his Kindle to the spine of his precious first edition. After a while, the words on the screen grew fuzzy.

He leaned his head back in his recliner and shut his eyes to rest them for a few minutes. A faint, comforting whiff from the sweet pages of his books lulled him into a state of relaxation and contentment. In this moment, all was right with the world.

A cold draft chilled his skin, raising goosebumps. He didn't bother opening his eyes. His chair sat beneath a vent and sometimes a large gust of wind blew into the ventilation, causing a draft. Minutes later, a weight built upon his chest, making it hard to breathe.

Now that he couldn't explain away.

His eyes flew open as his heart sped. No one else stood in the room with him, yet he struggled to lift his head and straighten his spine against the invisible but present weight pressing on his chest.

Could it be a panic attack? A sudden onset of asthma? A heart attack? Should he call an ambulance?

Davis pushed his stockinged feet against the carpet, pressing against the resistance keeping him in the chair, and stood. He took a step forward and the pressure on his chest vanished. Inhaling a deep breath, he ran his hands along his front, massaging the skin above his lungs.

For some reason, his skin hurt to the touch.

No longer winded, he rushed into the bathroom and turned on the light. He stood in front of the mirror and lifted his shirt. Two big red handprints stood out against his clammy, pale skin and a smattering of curly, light brown chest hair.

Michelle Godard-Richer

What the hell?

Davis rubbed his eyes. The handprints on his chest couldn't be real. His tired eyes had conjured them after the effects of working on a computer all day, then reading on a screen for hours. Sleep would cure him of such a ridiculous vision. In the morning, all would be well.

Chapter Four

DAVIS' head throbbed and a foul metallic taste coated his tongue. He kept his eyes shut to try to adjust to the pain in his head. He couldn't possibly be hungover when he hadn't imbibed anything alcoholic. It must be a horrible virus of some kind.

He cracked one eye open. Swirling, gray clouds filled the sky outside his bedroom window saving him from facing the sun's brutal light. A rainy day inside would be a blessing with how horrible he felt.

A weight rested on his chest. He shifted and a book slid down his body and landed in his bed. *No!* It wasn't just any book. It was his new treasure, *The Turn of the Screw*. Gently, he picked it up and flipped it over. The dust jacket appeared to be in the same condition as it was the previous night. He set it in the middle of his bed. With the swimming sensation in his head, he didn't trust himself to make it to the bookshelf in the sitting room without incident.

His legs wobbled as he stood. He stepped on something round. His foot went out from under him, and he stumbled forward, landing on his hands and knees. Thankfully, the thick carpet absorbed his fall, but he'd landed in something wet.

Due to his obsessive need for order, his house embodied

cleanliness, and he left nothing on the floor. With the pain in his head, standing would hurt. He stayed on his hands and knees and turned, searching for the object that tripped him. The neck of a familiar bottle peeked out from beneath his bed. With shaky hands, he grabbed it and pulled it out.

How did his bottle of bourbon end up in his bedroom while he slept? Worse, the bottle was empty, and it had been half full. He didn't remember drinking and as far as he knew, he'd never had issues with sleepwalking, yet he had the biggest hangover of all time.

Whatever had taken place the previous night had to be a one-time thing. A bizarre anomaly, and one that he wouldn't be repeating. If he never set his eyes on alcohol again it would be too soon.

Davis stood slowly trying to avoid a blood rush to his sore head. His head throbbed, but he managed to get to his feet again without sharp, shooting pains. The room tilted as he made his way to the bathroom and turned the shower on. The strong minty flavor of his toothpaste turned his stomach, but he withstood it to rid himself of the appalling taste in his mouth.

He swallowed pain relievers with a small mouthful of water and willed them to stay down. After a hot shower, the throbbing sensation in his head subsided, and a steady and more bearable pain remained. He used his towel to wipe condensation off the mirror. Studying his reflection, he discovered something else remained—two bruises in the shape of handprints on his chest.

Goosebumps rose along his skin and his teeth chattered as the stench of fear filled the room. Maybe the stress from all the screaming customers had caught up to him, causing his mind to break with reality. To fight off the chills, whether from the cold or fear, he tugged on his bathrobe, then headed for the kitchen.

At the end of the hallway, he stopped and let loose a string of curses. A floor lamp had fallen into his palm tree, knocking it over, and spilling dirt all over the floor. A bowl rested upside down on the dining room table and a puddle of something brown trickled out, dripping off the tabletop and onto the area rug below.

Worst of all was the mysterious yellow puddle on the middle cushion of the sofa.

Oh no! My other books!

He half ran, half stumbled around the corner into the sitting room, then let out a massive sigh. That room remained untouched, and his precious books were safe. Unable to accept that he could possibly be responsible for the mess, he moved from room to room, searching for a possible intruder.

He found no one, yet he would swear he sensed eyes crawling over him. Paranoia. Another sign of mental distress.

What's happening to me?

As uneasy as the messes all over his house made him, he couldn't tackle them properly in his current weakened state. Back in the kitchen, he popped two slices of bread in the toaster and brewed a pot of coffee. While the bread toasted, he collected dirty glasses and plates from his nighttime escapades and placed them in the dishwasher.

He took his phone off the charger and entered his passcode. Thankfully, he hadn't sent out a bunch of drunken text messages to anyone. He had a new message from Esme.

— *How's your weekend going?* —

She'd also sent a photo of her and her friend at the spa with cucumber slices over their eyes and mud on their faces.

He lied. — *I'm fine. Enjoy your weekend at the spa.* —

If only she'd picked a different weekend for their spa getaway. He needed her. But she needed to relax and escape all the horrible media attention surrounding her father. Since the story of her gruesome discovery broke, the media hounded her nonstop. They staked out her apartment building and the salon she worked at. It would die down for a few days only to intensify every time the police confirmed another victim's identity.

Her sister Lucy, on the other hand, enjoyed the attention. She gave tearful interviews apologizing to the families and expressing her condolences. *Crocodile tears.* She posted the same types of things on social media, amassing a ton of followers. She'd used their father's crimes to become a local celebrity.

Davis believed in karma. Eventually, Lucy's behavior would come back to bite her in the butt.

He took his toast and coffee to the dining room and found a non-sticky area to rest his plate and mug. While chewing, he glanced around the house at all the messes. He couldn't help but wonder what he did, or didn't do, to get to this point. Whatever was plaguing him, he would deal with it. One minute at a time, one task at a time to clean up the mess, and one day at a time.

Chapter Five

By dinnertime Davis' headache was gone, and his house was back to its usual meticulous state. If it weren't for the bruises on his chest, he could almost forget the horrible happenings of that morning.

He'd tried positioning his own hands over the marks, but it wasn't possible to bend his wrists with his fingers pointing towards his face to line up with the bruises. He opened his notebook computer and typed handprint bruises into the search bar.

The first few pages of results gave the obvious yet impossible answer of someone pushing you hard. He continued scrolling until he came upon a few search results listing a different and less plausible explanation. Large bruises from unexplained sources could be left behind by a ghost.

Davis laughed, then shuddered at the edge of lunacy in the sound of his own laughter. Having never been proven to exist, ghosts must be a figment of one's imagination. If he had to wager a guess, people experiencing psychotic breaks, like he had that morning, used the notion of ghosts to justify their experiences rather than owning up to them.

But he couldn't stop other thoughts from creeping into his

mind. The pressure on his chest the previous night. The creepy crow in the front yard. The shadows shifting in his peripheral vision, and the eyes he sensed upon him this very moment.

His parents raised him as a Catholic, but unless he was home with them over the holidays, he never attended church. With the bizarre happenings in his house, a church would be a good place to clear his head. St. Francis was only a few streets away, and on a Saturday evening, there would be Mass. He searched the times on his computer. Mass would begin at 6:30. If he hurried, he could make it.

He changed into black chinos and a sweater, then slipped on sneakers and his wool coat. Outside his front door, the brisk, fall air greeted him. Wings flapped overhead, then a black crow landed on the edge of his roof.

Caw! Razzhole!

Davis tore his eyes away from the crow's beady gaze and ran up the driveway to the sidewalk. He didn't dare look behind him to see if the demented, cursing bird followed. Once he'd put a few blocks between him and his house, he chanced a look behind him. Thankfully, no crows perched in the trees.

He inhaled a deep breath of refreshing cool air. *I'm being ridiculous.*

Mass started in ten minutes. With his hands in his pockets, he strode along the sidewalk. The farther he got from his house, the lighter his steps became. The exercise cleared the last lingering remnants of fog from his brain.

Davis stepped inside the church, dipped his fingers in holy water, and made the sign of the cross while reciting a prayer in his head for forgiveness. He still wasn't convinced karma or anything he'd done had led to the craziness of the previous night, but it didn't hurt to cover all his bases.

Despite the discomfort of the wooden pew, a sense of calm loosened the tension in his neck and shoulders. His eyelids grew heavy as the minister gave the sermon, and he struggled to stay awake. If only he could sleep on the pew in the sanctuary of the church rather than alone in his own bed. Although the likelihood of a repeat of the previous night was low.

After Mass, he would return home to his own bed in his own house, and everything would be fine.

Chapter Six

DAVIS OPENED HIS EYES, thankful not to be hungover. But for some odd reason, *The Turn of the Screw* leaned against the extra pillow on the other side of his bed. He'd placed it on the shelf the previous day during his cleaning spree. How had it gotten to his bedroom again?

A familiar coppery scent filled the air, but he couldn't place it. The closed curtains muted the daylight outside the window. He reached for his phone on the bedside table to check the time, then paused with his hand in the air.

He scrambled into a sitting position.

No! This can't be happening!

His hands, his pajamas, the bedsheets, and the carpet—all covered in droplets of blood. Air burst in and out of his lungs at a frantic pace as he stripped his clothes off, then ran to the bathroom.

He scrubbed his hands and arms as well as the blood spatter on his face, then searched his body for the source of the bleeding. He would've had to cut himself badly enough to make such a mess. The tiny cuts on his hands and wrists weren't there when he went to bed, but they couldn't have bled that much.

If the blood didn't come from him, then where had it come from? Worse, who did it belong to?

What have I done?

His rubbery legs made it difficult to remain standing. He leaned against the wall and dropped into a sitting position. In an effort to rein in the overwhelming urge to panic, he wrapped his arms around his knees and squeezed.

He'd never hurt anyone in his life. He abhorred violence. Sleepwalking or not, he couldn't picture himself injuring another person. Maybe he'd stopped to help someone else with their injury? Either way, he needed to assume the worst and deal with the mess.

Focus.

What did he need to do next? One minute at a time and one task at a time. That plan had worked during his waking hours the previous day and it would work now.

Given someone else's blood trailed around his house, his priority had to be to get rid of the evidence. In case the police came calling, he'd burn his pajamas and sheets in the fireplace, then he'd bleach the whole house.

After that, he needed to get his hands on a ton of energy drinks because he wouldn't be sleeping until Esme got back from her trip and could keep an eye on him. Figuring out what to tell her would be another conundrum. The truth wasn't an option.

They'd only been together six months. With her father being a killer, she'd head for the hills, or the police station, if she found out he'd woken covered in someone else's blood. She hadn't hesitated to rat out her father. Until he saw a psychiatrist and started medication for the sleepwalking, he couldn't trust himself to sleep unsupervised.

He shut his eyes and breathed in deeply, readying himself to clean his house again. Before facing the main living area and whatever messes he may discover, he stripped his sheets off his bed. Thankfully, the fabric had absorbed the blood. The mattress didn't show signs of staining, but he spritzed it with bleach anyway to be on the safe side.

By some miracle, *The Turn of the Screw* didn't have a single drop of blood on it.

Clad in only his boxers from the previous day, he bundled his bloody tee and jeans inside his sheets, carried them to the fireplace in the living room, and started a fire. The acrid odor of the burning fabric along with the scent of the wood wasn't awful, but it wasn't aromatic either. He opened the windows to air out the house.

The living and dining rooms appeared undisturbed from his nightly exploits. But his sneakers hadn't fared as well, and a bloody trail of his footprints led from the front door to his bedroom.

His comforter only had a bit of blood on it, so he sprayed it with stain remover and threw it in the wash with his sneakers and a capful of bleach.

Wait, hold on a second.

If his shoes left a bloody trail in the house, it stood to reason they left a trail to the door. He opened the front door a crack and peered outside. By some miracle the porch, stairs, and driveway were wet. The rain in the night had taken care of that problem for him, but he should probably spray the ground with bleach as a precaution.

If he missed one drop of blood, it could lead to questions he couldn't answer. Oh, God. And if he had done something, he needed to pray no one saw or caught him on camera. Unfortunately, he couldn't control that.

He filled a bucket with hot water and bleach and pulled on rubber gloves, then scrubbed the carpet in the hallway and bedroom with a scrub brush. After an hour, he couldn't see any visible stains. As a precaution, he used his spot carpet cleaning machine to go over the whole area, sucking up the dirty water.

With all the blood cleaned up, his adrenaline waned, and he yawned. He peeled off the rubber gloves. A nap would be perfect except he couldn't sleep and risk another incident. Instead, he lathered his dry, red hands in moisturizer, then bundled up to drive to the store for those energy drinks.

The rain had stopped, but the heavy, dark gray clouds in the sky threatened more rain. Davis pushed the button on his key fob to unlock his Mustang, then opened the driver's door. The same coppery smell from earlier smacked him in the face. Half-dry droplets of blood rested on the leather seat and the steering wheel.

Panic tightened around his throat and tears prickled his eyes. The severity of the situation smacked him in the face. Not only did he have more blood to clean, but he'd graduated from sleep-walking to sleep drinking, to sleep driving, and possibly sleep attacking and/or killing.

Davis hurried inside and grabbed his spray bottle of diluted bleach and a cloth. He moved the seat backwards and forwards, sprayed every inch of the carpet with the bleach solution, then went over it again with his small shampooer. In an attempt to put the blood out of his mind, he tucked his supplies away.

The clouds opened as he ran to his car. He turned on the radio, then backed out of the driveway. The announcer's voice blared through the sound system.

Breaking news. The body of a woman whose identity has not yet been released was discovered earlier this morning in a home on Elm Street. Police are on the scene.

Davis trembled so hard, he struggled to hang onto the steering wheel. He pulled over to the curb then turned off the radio. He didn't want his mind to jump to the conclusion that he had something to do with the woman's death. But how could he not think it?

Chapter Seven

Somehow, despite the shocking news on the radio, Davis managed to get energy drinks and drive home without losing control of his mind or his Mustang. He sat on the couch, prepared to endure a long and lonely day and night. His phone rang as he popped the tab on an energy drink, and a picture of Esme flashed on the screen.

He answered, "Hey, how's the spa trip?"

"I'm on my way home. Something awful happened. It's Lucy."

"What about her?"

Esme sobbed. "She's dead. Someone murdered her last night. My mom just identified her body at the morgue. Some sicko copycat strangled her and yanked her teeth out."

His stomach tightened and his guts liquified. *What if I...no, I didn't do it.* "That's horrible! I'm so sorry. Do you want to meet at your apartment? I'm sure you don't want to be alone."

The television flicked on by itself in front of him. The local news channel came on, and a picture of Lucy filled the screen. He scrambled for the remote on the table next to the couch and hit the mute button. Out of the corner of his eye, a shadow dashed by. His chest heaved as he gasped for air, then stood and spun in a circle, searching the room.

No one, yet he would swear eyes crawled over his skin.

Esme's voice came through his phone. "I'm headed to my mom's house. Would you come over and stay there with me?"

The idea of staying at Esme's mother's house under such insane and sad circumstances didn't appeal to him, but neither did staying in his house after all the bizarre happenings. He glanced around the room. A change in scenery would do him good. But what if he sleepwalked again? Esme slept light enough to notice. He'd have to risk it. "Of course, I will. Text me when you get there. Drive carefully. You probably shouldn't be driving."

"Don't worry. I'm fine. I'll see you later. I love you."

"I love you, too." Davis hung up and stared at the television.

He lowered his head on his folded hands and prayed the police would arrest someone else. Then he could set aside the crazy notion that he'd murdered his girlfriend's sister. He'd never liked Lucy, but he didn't wish her dead. How horribly sad for Esme and her mother. They'd already been through too much with all the negative attention rained upon them by being related to Peter McFadden.

Later that day, Davis parked and slung his overnight bag over his shoulder. He carried three orders of chicken soup with bread to the front door of Mary Engelbert's tiny bungalow. The sense of unease plaguing him at home dissipated as it had the previous evening when he'd attended church. It taunted him with a sliver of hope that his night escapades might not happen again.

With his stomach in knots, he couldn't manage anything too substantial for dinner and he imagined the women felt the same. Murder has a way of killing an appetite.

Esme opened the door with a tiny, sad smile on her face and swollen, red eyes. "I'm so glad you're here."

"I brought soup and bread." He kissed her cheek. "How are you holding up?"

She took the bag from him. "I've never cried this much, but I guess I'm okay."

He glanced around the small living room as she led him to the empty kitchen. "How's Mary?"

She unpacked two containers of soup and the bread, then stuck the other portion of soup in the fridge. "My mom is a crying zombie now, but that's to be expected. I tucked her into bed a little while ago. Earlier, she was in a rage. She blames my dad. She thinks it's either someone getting revenge for what he did, or that he drew the attention of a copycat to Lucy."

He removed the lids and doled out the plastic cutlery. The aromatic thyme and chicken scent the soup gave off didn't entice him to eat it the way it normally did. "She's probably right. And Lucy drew attention to herself with all the social media posts and media interviews. Whereas you've kept a low profile, but you shouldn't be alone. If it's connected to your father, then you might be in danger."

"Oh, God. I didn't think that far ahead. You're right. And those stupid reporters probably posted footage of my apartment building while they were camped out there."

He blew on a spoonful of soup. "And your mother's house. Did the police say they'd keep an eye on this place?"

"I don't know. Will you stay here until the police catch the killer?"

What if the killer is me? His throat thickened and he swallowed hard to get the soup in his mouth to go down. Staying at Mary's would keep the police away from his house if they happened to want to talk to Esme. He'd bleached everything but police technology was sophisticated. "I'll do my best, but I have to work."

She ripped a piece off her bread. "I figured. Me too. I only get five bereavement days, and there's so much to do. We have to wait for an autopsy before they release Lucy's body, so we can't make any arrangements."

"Under the circumstances, you'd think the salon would give you longer."

"They will, but unpaid. This really sucks. My sister was a little selfish sometimes, but she had a heart of gold and only wanted the best for people she cared about. She didn't deserve this."

"No, she didn't." He never liked Lucy, but murder went a lot further than the karma headed her way.

Hours ticked by and Mary didn't emerge from her room. Davis curled up with Esme in the guest room, dreading the idea of sleeping. He issued a silent prayer as his eyelids grew heavy that nothing horrible would happen, and he clung to Esme for dear life.

Chapter Eight

THE NEXT MORNING, Davis opened his eyes to find himself in a strange room. It took a minute for him to remember he'd slept in the guest room with Esme. She wasn't there, but she'd probably gotten up to check on her mother. Esme's kindness was unwavering to those she cared about.

No traces of blood clung to his hands or pajamas, and his head didn't feel like it had swollen to double its size. He dared to hope he'd made it through the night without sleepwalking and doing anything insane. The faster he found Esme, the sooner he'd know for sure. He took a quick shower in the adjoining bathroom, banging both his elbows on the walls of the tiny shower stall multiple times. Then dressed quickly and set out to find his hosts.

The aroma of coffee lured him to the kitchen. Esme sat alone at the peninsula with a somber expression on her face. Her fingers traced the grout lines of the forest green tile countertop.

He perched on the stool beside her. "Hey, how are things?"

"Mom doesn't want to get out of bed, and she wants to be alone. I brought her coffee and toast. I figured it would be best to let her grieve in her own way. At least for now."

"You're doing the right thing. Everyone grieves in their own way. Did you want me to go out and get us something for breakfast?"

She shrugged. "I'm not hungry, but I don't mind making you some eggs."

He rubbed her shoulder. "You should try to eat something. You barely touched your soup at dinner."

"I will a bit later."

The doorbell rang, interrupting their conversation.

"Not again. I can't deal with this." Esme slouched and rested her elbows on the counter. "Two of the neighbors came by this morning while you were in bed. One left lasagna and the other a chicken casserole."

Davis stood and rested a hand on her shoulder. "People mean well. Cooking can be a chore when you're sad and depressed."

"It's not the neighbors that are upsetting. There are media vans outside again, trying to interview people. Earlier, I yelled at them to fuck off. I hope they don't play a clip of that later."

"I'll get it." He took a deep breath to keep his anxiety from taking control. Away from work, he avoided people, especially people he didn't know.

He put his eye to the peephole, and his control slipped a little. Two men in suits stood on the porch with badges clipped to their belts and unreadable expressions on their faces. Cops. A fresh salt and pepper haircut showed one man's middle age, and the other's face was unwrinkled and had his hair in a neat ponytail.

Relax. They can't be here for me.

He opened the door. "Hello, Officers. Come in." He stepped back and an awkward silence spread. Under the circumstances, he figured it better to stay quiet rather than risk talking too much and making himself appear guilty.

The older police officer broke the silence. "I'm Detective Swanson, and this is Detective Patterson. We're here to speak to Mary Engelbert."

Esme approached them. "My mother's been in bed since last night. I don't think she's in any shape to speak to you right now.

Didn't you ask her a bunch of questions at the police station yesterday?"

Detective Patterson said, "Well, maybe you can help us then. Could you answer some questions?"

"I don't know how much help I'll be, but I'll try." Esme turned and headed towards the old floral print sofa in the living room. "This way."

Davis didn't know whether to follow and sit next to Esme or make himself scarce. He didn't want to appear as if he meant to hide anything or avoid the police.

Esme met his gaze with an expression of longing and made the decision for him.

Davis sat next to her and held her hand in his sweaty one. He needed the comfort and he wanted to comfort Esme. What a shitty situation.

Detective Swanson opened a small notebook. "You would be Esme Engelbert. Is that correct?"

"Yes."

Detective Swanson asked, "Can you think of anyone who would've wanted to hurt your sister? An ex-boyfriend? Someone she had a falling out with?"

Esme sighed. "My sister didn't have a filter, and she would say whatever came to mind. But she was a good person. I don't think the killer was someone she knew. After we discovered our father was the Colorado Strangler, she took advantage of the situation to get more social media followers. I'm guessing she attracted the wrong sort of people."

Detective Swanson scribbled notes. "We'll look into her social media accounts. Would you happen to have her passcode to her phone? It'll give us quicker access to her accounts."

Esme nodded. "It's 9876."

The edge came off Davis' anxiety. Thankfully, Esme agreed with the theory he'd put forward to her earlier on the phone, and now the police seemed interested in that angle. He believed it could be possible, despite the timing of when he woke covered in blood. The possibility still remained that he'd gotten in a brawl outside a bar while sleepwalking. If he found the shameless way Lucy had used her father's death offensive, then others probably did too.

Esme asked, "Do you have any leads?"

Detective Swanson said, "We're looking into a few things. We can't be more specific with an active investigation. Where were you Saturday night?"

Esme narrowed her eyes. "I spent the night with my friend Shelley at a spa resort. I can give you her number and the number of the spa."

Detective Patterson broke his silence. "So, that means you weren't with your boyfriend here. Sorry, we didn't catch your name, sir."

Crap. "I'm Davis Shetland."

Detective Patterson said, "Where were *you* on Saturday night?"

Isn't that the million-dollar question? "In my bed sleeping. I'm afraid no one can verify since I live alone in a single-dwelling home."

Detective Swanson continued scrawling in his notebook. "How well did you know the victim?"

Davis opened his mouth to respond.

But Esme beat him to it. "He hardly knows her. I introduced them a month ago when we met for drinks. Beyond that, we haven't spent any time with her together."

Davis nodded. "That's the only time I've ever seen Lucy besides the brief news clips. It saddens me that I never really got a chance to know her."

Detective Patterson pulled out his phone, tapped on the screen a few times, and held it out to Esme. "We have some grainy footage of a man leaving her townhouse captured on a neighbor's camera across the street. Do you recognize him?"

Davis' heart pounded in his eardrums. This could be his worst nightmare come true. But surely if the police recognized him in the footage, they would've arrested him already. He leaned his head next to Esme's shoulder as she pressed play.

In the grainy, dark footage, someone strode out Lucy's front door wearing a black baseball cap pulled down with their neck scrunched up to hide their face, a black puffer coat, and dark pants. With their face hidden from view, the forensics team could sharpen and zoom in on the footage, but it still wouldn't be enough to identify the culprit.

Davis had the same average height and medium build as the person in the video, but so did many other men and some taller women. He didn't own caps, but he did own a black puffer coat, and he had burned a pair of bloody dark jeans in his fireplace. During his cleaning escapade, he hadn't thought to check the coats on the hook by the front door.

Esme studied the footage. "I'm sorry. I wish I could help, but I have no idea who this is."

Davis did his best to keep his tone even instead of fearful or raised. "Me neither."

Detective Swanson met Davis' gaze and said nothing. Davis' skin crawled under the detective's scrutiny, but he wouldn't be the one to look away first as if he had something to hide.

Detective Patterson collected his phone, breaking the awkward silence. "All right, then. We'll be going."

Detective Swanson handed Esme his card. "If you think of anything else we should know, give me a call. The ME will be in touch to release your sister's remains soon, and we'll have someone drop off the keys to her apartment when the crime scene techs are done later today. We'll show ourselves out."

Esme's puffy eyes filled with tears, and she nodded.

Davis wrapped an arm around her. "I'm sorry you're going through this."

She leaned into him, resting her head on his shoulder. "This is a nightmare that's never-ending. How do you grieve and recover from something like this? She died a violent death. And until they figure out who killed her, it'll be like an open wound that will never heal."

He wrapped his arms around her. "I'm so sorry for your loss. They say time heals all wounds, but I don't think that's true. The sting should fade with time, but you'll never forget your sister and what happened."

If that video was all the police had, they may never figure out who killed Lucy. If he did it, then he didn't want to be discovered, but he'd much rather learn that someone else had murdered Lucy. The guilt, even with no recollection of killing her, weighed on him as if he carried the whole world on his back.

How could this have happened?

Chapter Nine

GRIEF ZAPPED every bit of Esme's energy. The comfort of Davis' presence had gotten her out of bed that morning and kept her from giving up on life like her mother had. His arms around her after the police visit reminded her that no matter how downright miserable things were now, she had something to live for.

Because of that, she needed to snap herself out of her funk and check on her mother again. After all her mother had been through, she'd find the strength to surface from her grief. With her horrible father dead, and now her sister, all that remained of their family unit was each other.

She let go of Davis and got to her feet. "Want some of the chicken casserole the neighbor dropped off? Thanks to the police we missed breakfast, and Mom really needs to eat. She didn't touch her soup last night. I'm worried about her."

"Sure. I'll keep you company in the kitchen."

"I'm glad you're here." Esme spooned some casserole into a bowl and stuck it in the microwave.

Davis wasn't much of a talker, but he seemed quieter than usual and preoccupied. Maybe he didn't know what to say? He'd clung to her the night before in bed, not normal behavior for him, but she appreciated the sweet gesture of comfort.

She liked his cute, boy next door looks with his medium build and dark hair and eyes, as well as his dependable, boring job. But what she loved about him was his personality. Unlike her supposed friends, he didn't look at her like she was a piranha after news about her father broke.

Maybe that's why Lucy had done all the interviews and social media posts, so people wouldn't treat her like gum on the bottom of their shoe. But it had the opposite effect. Poor Lucy. She shuddered. What if Davis was right and the killer wanted to kill her and her mother too?

Esme opened the microwave, and the aroma of the chicken and vegetables comforted her. The familiar scent didn't make her hungry with her stomach twisted in knots, but it was the type of meal her mother had cooked on so many occasions over the years, triggering memories of happier times. Maybe it would comfort her mother in the same way.

She carried the food to her mother's room. "Mom, I brought some chicken casserole."

Her mother rolled over to face her. "I wish you would've let me sleep." Agitation crept into the tone of her voice. "When I'm sleeping, I can forget. I need to forget."

"Mom, you need to eat. Then you can go back to sleep again. You didn't eat all day yesterday, remember? And you didn't eat the toast I brought this morning."

"Has it been that long?"

Esme nodded.

"Sorry, if I was a bit snappy. I didn't realize." Her mother shifted into a sitting position and took the bowl of food. "I love you. And I appreciate that you want to stay here and take care of me, but I need to be alone for a few days. I need to veg on the couch or in bed in my pajamas and ignore the world. I know Davis will take care of you. So, can you give me two days of solitude? Then I think I'll be able to face people again."

She didn't want to leave her mother alone, but she also didn't want to deny her wishes. "If that's what you want, Mom. I'll shower, and then I'll go stay with Davis. But you need to promise me you'll eat. And lock the door. The killer is still out there."

"I promise. I'll be fine. We've been through a lot, and we'll get through this."

Esme sighed as a tremendous wave of relief came over her at her mother's words. Thank heavens her mother was surfacing and showing signs of being able to cope. "We will, Mom. I'll be there. Whatever you need me to do."

"You seem to be holding up better than I am, but if you need me, call."

"I'll be okay. Don't worry about me, and I love you too." Esme left her mother in peace and closed the bedroom door.

Davis stood nearby in the hallway, taking clinging to a new level, and making her feel as if the walls were closing in.

She took him by the elbow and guided him into her room, shutting the door behind them. "Were you eavesdropping?"

His pupils grew. "I'm sorry. I wanted to be nearby in case you needed something. I didn't realize you wanted privacy."

"It's not a big deal, but I'd rather you didn't in the future. My mom would've been angry if she saw you lingering outside her room."

"It won't happen again. I promise. Is she...do you think it's me she wants gone?"

"No, she would've said so. I think she just needs space. Are you okay with going back to your place?"

He pursed his lips and hesitated. "We could. Are you sure you wouldn't rather stay at your apartment?"

"If you don't want to be around me either, just say so."

He held her shoulders. "No, no. Nothing like that. I swear. I just thought you'd be more comfortable in your own space."

"Why would you want to stay at my crappy apartment with the paper-thin walls when you have a nice, clean, and quiet house? We always stay at your place."

"Right, my place it is then. I'd love to have you there."

"Okay."

He seemed genuine in his desire for her to stay, yet he hesitated, and she sensed there was more to the situation. He was holding something back. Whatever it was, she'd get it out of him.

Chapter Ten

After one night's reprieve from the sleepwalking, Davis pulled into his driveway and inhaled a shaky breath. His knuckles throbbed from how tightly he'd clutched the steering wheel on the way over from Mary's house.

He kept replaying the bloody mess from the previous morning in his head along with the video the detective showed them. He found it harder and harder to believe he hadn't killed Lucy. Yet how could he commit such a horrific crime and have no memory of it?

None of it made sense. Neither did the bruises on his chest, the shadow shifting around his house, and the television turning itself on in time for a segment on Lucy's murder. The internet search suggested a ghost, but he couldn't help but wonder about his sanity.

Esme pulled in behind him and parked. Thankfully, she'd wanted to take her own car. It gave him a chance to prepare to face his house and the prospect of sleeping in his own bed again. He desperately wanted to tell her about the sleepwalking and warn her to wake him, but he also didn't want to chase her away.

He climbed out of the car and took Esme's bag from her. "I'll carry it."

"Thank you. You're such a gentleman."

"No problem." An ominous flutter of wings passed over his head.

Caw! "Razzhole!"

Esme grabbed his arm. "Holy shit! It's Ezekiel. How did he find me here?"

"You know that creepy bird? He was here when I got home Friday."

"He was my father's pet. He kept him in a big cage."

How bizarre that Peter's bird first appeared less than an hour after Davis bought his book. "That's a freaky coincidence. How did he get loose?"

"I couldn't take him home because of the no-pet rule in my building, and Lucy, of course, wouldn't take him. My father used to let him fly around the forest when they went camping all the time, so I figured he'd be happier free."

"He makes me uneasy. Let's go in."

Esme followed him inside, then wrinkled her nose as she hung her coat on the rack. "I smell bleach."

He'd anticipated her question and had an excuse at the ready. He hated lying, but he had no choice. "I stayed up too long reading the other night and got drowsy. I dribbled soda all over the carpet from my reading chair to beside my bed."

She chuckled and a smile graced her lips for the first time in ages. "That had to be horrifying for you with how much of a clean freak you are."

"It was. And I had no one to blame but myself."

A loud voice blasted out of the living room, interrupting their conversation.

Davis rounded the corner. Once again, the television had turned itself on. He strode to the coffee table, clutched the remote, and hit the power button.

Esme stood nearby. "Did the TV turn itself on? I mean, I think we would've heard it when we first came inside, right?"

"There must be a loose wire in the television or something. It happened while I was talking to you on the phone yesterday."

"Maybe. It's odd though. You never watch television with the volume up that high."

Davis shrugged. "If it keeps happening, I'll have to get a new one is all." Although, she made a valid point. He didn't want to agree with her and feed into the creepy atmosphere. "Would you like some tea? Maybe we could try watching a movie if the TV cooperates."

"Sure, that would be nice. Thank you."

He set to work filling the kettle.

Esme brought out the mugs and the box of teabags. "I feel guilty doing something normal like this when my sister never will again. I'd like to believe she's in a better place."

Guilt made the chicken casserole they'd eaten sit like a rock in his stomach. "There are a lot of good things in this life along with the bad, but I'd like to believe what people say who've had near death experiences about feeling no pain while finding a white light." A light he may never see if he'd sent Lucy to meet their maker.

Time roared by the way it usually did when you didn't want it to slow down. The afternoon bled into the evening until the moon lorded over the sky, signaling an end to the daytime. Soon, bedtime would come, and he couldn't escape it.

Chapter Eleven

Esme's eyes opened and while they adjusted to Davis' dark bedroom, she rolled over and groped the space in the bed beside her. No Davis. He slept hard and seldom woke in the middle of the night. Normally, she'd wait for him to return to bed, but something told her she should seek him out.

She climbed out of bed and the lingering odor of bleach crept up her nose, bringing back memories she'd rather forget. Mostly, from all the time she'd spent in the hospital during her mother's illness.

Off-key singing came from the main living area. The voice sounded a bit like Davis, and oddly, also like someone else, but she couldn't place it. She'd never heard him sing before. Maybe Davis sounded like that all the time.

At the end of the hallway, she rounded the corner into the kitchen. Davis stood leaning against the kitchen counter with an open jar of peanut butter and a spoon. Closer to him, she could make out the words of his song, and the fine hairs on her arms raised.

Without missing a single word, he was singing "Hotel California" by the Eagles. Her father's favorite song. And her father also used to eat peanut butter straight from the jar. It could be a bizarre coincidence, like Ezekiel appearing outside the house, and Davis' television troubles. But at what point did too many freaky events combine to become something else, something more sinister? This situation reeked like her father.

"Davis?"

He didn't react or miss a word of the song as he stared, unblinking, in the same direction. Was he sleepwalking?

Her hands shook, and instinct told her to run away from his house and never return. But she loved Davis, and his behavior was probably her fault by association for having such an ass for a father.

"Dad?"

Davis swiveled his head toward her, then laughed in her face. "Well, isn't it my favorite daughter. We have so much in common. Don't we?"

"No! We *don't*. I'm not an asshole like you." She grabbed Davis by the shoulders and shook him hard. "Wake up!"

Davis blinked and then his eyes locked on hers. "Esme?" He glanced at his hands, then set the jar of peanut butter and the spoon on the counter beside *The Turn of the Screw*. Whenever these things happened, the book was always nearby.

Oh, no! It happened again.

At least he'd only been eating peanut butter this time. He'd have to do something tomorrow to stop the sleepwalking. He needed professional help in the form of some strong pills.

Esme's eyes were larger than usual. "You don't remember coming into the kitchen or eating peanut butter, and singing "Hotel California," do you?"

"What? No. I must've been hungry from us not eating much with everything that's been going on." Singing? He never sang.

"Have you ever sleepwalked before?"

He couldn't bring himself to confess he might've killed her

sister. "I...I don't think so. It must be the stress. Work has been getting to me more lately, too. Difficult clients."

"It's not safe, Davis. You need to get help for this. What if you went for a walk and got hit by a car, or tried to cook and set the house on fire?"

He frowned. "You're right. I'll call around for a doctor's appointment tomorrow and get a prescription."

"Can you do something for me?"

"I'll try."

"Sing that song again."

"What song?"

""Hotel California.""

He couldn't talk his way around that question. "I can't. I don't know the words."

"That's what I was afraid of." Her bottom lip quivered. "I'm not sure a prescription can help you."

"Of course, it can."

"We need a medium or a priest. My father is haunting you. Shit, maybe he's even possessing you. It's my fault. None of our boyfriends were ever good enough in his eyes."

"That's ridiculous." He scoffed half-heartedly on the outside while burying the panic inside as it clawed at his stomach. If Peter was possessing him, he could've forced him to murder Lucy. But why would he kill his own daughter?

"Is it? Then explain why you were singing my father's favorite song, a song you don't know while eating peanut butter from a jar like he used to. Why did you respond when I called you Dad? And why did Ezekiel show up here? You never met my father or his bird."

"I can't explain it." As she made her case, it became harder and harder to deny his problems were of a paranormal nature. But was it because of Esme? Or was Peter angry with him for buying his book? If he told her about *The Turn of the Screw*, she'd make him get rid of it. After searching for a decent copy of that book for ten years, he didn't want to give it up. If they got a priest to bless the house, then it should cleanse the book. He flipped on the kitchen light and lifted his t-shirt. "I can't explain this either."

She traced the yellow bruises in the shape of handprints on his chest. "Christ. When did this happen?"

"Friday night. When I was reading, I felt pressure on my chest. The next morning, I woke up and discovered these bruises."

Esme narrowed her eyes. "Why didn't you tell me?"

"You had enough on your plate with Lucy. We'll look for help first thing tomorrow."

"A priest from my mother's church came by the house and said to reach out if we needed anything. If you're okay with it, we'll visit him in the morning."

"Yes, I'm not too proud to admit the idea of your serial killer father taking over while I'm asleep is terrifying."

Crack!

Esme covered her mouth. "Oh, my God!"

Davis followed her gaze and spun. A huge crack ran up the glass of the mirror hanging beside the front door. "Well, if he's doing that, then he's not inside me, right?" Something heavy knocked him in the chest, and he stumbled back. "Ouch!"

She grabbed his arm, her fingers digging into his skin. "Are you okay?"

"I don't know. I think so. He just shoved me."

"Nothing happened at my mom's house, right?"

"No. Things only seem to happen here. Whenever I leave, I feel better. It's only midnight. Let's get a motel for the rest of the night."

Davis prided himself on remaining at an even keel. Trying to help frustrated clients with tech issues required extra patience. But his jaw tightened, and his muscles ached as he allowed Peter to chase him from his own house.

He sent up a silent prayer that the priest would believe them and send Peter McFadden packing.

Chapter Twelve

DAVIS AWOKE to sunlight seeping around the edges of the thin motel curtains. The light highlighted the threadbare carpet and dents in the yellowed walls that were cloaked in darkness the previous night. With how shaken he'd been, he'd stopped at the first hotel they'd come across.

Esme still had her leg draped across him and her arm around his chest. Almost as if she thought keeping hold of him would keep her father's ghost away. Maybe it had. He didn't sense him nearby. For some reason, Peter never followed him out of the house.

In the light of day, the idea of possession seemed preposterous, yet he'd done unexplainable things in his sleep with no memory of them. If he'd murdered Lucy while possessed by her father, that would absolve him of moral guilt. As long as the police couldn't pin the murder on him, he could get on with his life.

But if he hurt anyone else, with the awareness of the sleep-walking/possession happening, he wouldn't be able to forgive himself. If Esme hadn't woken when she did, what else would he have done besides eat peanut butter and sing a song he didn't know?

Before Friday the 13th, and the start of the creepy happenings, he'd found the idea of the paranormal absurd. He couldn't imagine ghosts, let alone possession, having any basis in reality. The concept of anything existing after death seemed improbable, but this experience had shaken his beliefs and restored his faith in the afterlife.

He wrapped an arm around Esme and prayed the nightmare would end soon so they could have a life together. He'd never find a more caring and loyal woman. After her life imploded, she cared for her mother despite her own suffering. And even though she seemed certain her father had possessed him, she stuck around instead of running.

She stirred.

He kissed her forehead. "Good morning."

She glanced around the room. "We made it through the night."

"Yes, we did."

They grabbed breakfast at a nearby diner, then Esme gave him directions to the church her mother attended. The heavy wooden doors to the main vestibule were locked.

Davis asked, "Would anyone be here on a Monday?"

"There should be someone in the office." She took his hand and led him around the side of the church to another door.

He knocked and waited with bated breath. At this point, he'd drive to every church in the city if he needed to.

The lock clicked, then the door opened. A priest wearing a clerical collar stood inside the entrance. "Hello, Esme. Come in. Who's your friend?"

Esme smiled. "This is my boyfriend, Davis. Father Micheal, we need your help."

Father Micheal gestured to two chairs in front of a desk. "Please sit."

Davis sat and met Esme's gaze, imploring her to explain. Since the priest knew her, it might be better coming from her.

Esme cleared her throat, and her voice trembled. "I know this is going to sound crazy, but my father is haunting Davis. Last night, I found Davis in the kitchen singing my father's favorite song, a song Davis doesn't know. I called him by his name, and he stared ahead blankly, but when I addressed him as my dad, he laughed in my face. I shook Davis hard, and when he snapped out of it, he had no memory of any of it."

Father Micheal shifted his gaze to Davis. "Do you have a history of sleepwalking?"

"No. Other bizarre things have also been happening. My television is turning itself on, I'm seeing shadows out of the corner of my eye, and a large mirror cracked with no explainable cause last night." It pained him to speak a half-truth to the priest, but he couldn't cop to a murder he suspected he committed.

Esme said, "Father, he has bruises on his chest in the shape of handprints."

Father Micheal pressed his long fingers together in the shape of a steeple. "I don't see Davis exhibiting any signs of possession. He entered the church without issue. If it makes you feel better, we can meet at your house this afternoon. I'll bless the whole house top to bottom and drive out any negative energies that may be present."

Davis grasped at the lifeline. "Yes, please, Father. That would be wonderful."

If this didn't work, then what?

Chapter Thirteen

DAVIS PARKED in his driveway and stared at the house with trepidation. Esme clutched her hands together in the passenger seat, seemingly in no hurry to go inside either. Ezekiel perched in his usual spot on the Rocky Mountain Juniper.

"What do you think your father will do when faced with the priest?"

"I don't know. He never talked about religion or went to church. Come to think of it, we found a few creepy, old occult books on his shelves. But he probably just bought them to add to his collection." She squeezed his hand. "I think what's most important is that we have faith in Father Micheal's blessing."

"You're right. We need to believe without a doubt that this will work."

He didn't want to knock Esme's confidence by voicing his concerns. What if her father left only to return after the priest's blessing wore off? The sinister spirit of a serial killer had to be harder to get rid of than your average ghost.

A grey sedan parked next to the curb in front of the house and Father Micheal climbed out.

Davis locked eyes with Esme and the bitter scent of shared fear spread between them. "Do you want to wait here?"

A spark filled her gaze as she opened the car door. "No. I'm not letting you deal with my father alone."

Davis followed her to the house, ignoring a crippling sense of dread. Peter McFadden had possessed him three times. What if each time it happened, Peter leeched a part of his soul away and grew stronger?

Father Micheal stood on the porch with a cross and a leather-wrapped, vintage Bible in his hands. The priest didn't show any outward signs of stress or fear. Did parishioners go to him with these types of strange tales on a regular basis? Did he agree to bless houses to soothe them while not really believing ghosts existed?

Davis did his best to smile at the priest. "Thank you again for coming, Father Micheal."

Father Micheal nodded. "You're welcome. Shall we?"

Davis unlocked the door and gestured for the priest to enter first.

Esme patted Davis' shoulder on the way inside.

After he shut the door behind them, a shiver ran along Davis' spine and a heaviness hung in the air.

Esme took Father Micheal's black wool coat and hung it on the coat rack on top of the jacket Davis had meant to examine for blood. She hung her dark blue puffer coat on a different hook. With all that had happened, he'd forgotten about the coat from the grainy video footage the police showed them.

Father Micheal handed his bible to Esme. "Hang onto this for me, please." He pulled a bottle of holy water from his pocket and held the cross in front of him. "Bless, O Lord God almighty..."

As the priest prayed, a quiet metallic grinding sound lingered in the background. A round, glass light fixture above Father Micheal dropped from the ceiling.

Davis lunged. "Father! Look up."

Father Micheal jumped out of the way. "Oh, my goodness!"

The fixture hit the floor and the glass shattered and the pieces scattered all over the entrance.

"I'm so sorry, Father." The three screws that had held it up pinged on the floor around Davis' feet.

The priest frowned, then glanced around the house. "Esme, my Bible please."

She gave the book to Father Micheal, then took a few steps backwards to where Davis stood and clasped his hand.

Davis wanted to tell her everything would be fine, but he didn't want to lie in front of the priest. Sinning couldn't be a good thing to do while trying to cleanse your house.

Father Micheal flipped through the Bible, then marked his page with a ribbon. He stepped into the living room and prayed with conviction. "The Lord is my shepherd; I shall not want. He makes me lie down in green pastures. He leads me beside still waters." The television turned on and blasted a game show at full volume. Father Micheal raised his voice and flicked holy water around the room. "He restores my soul. He leads me in paths of righteousness for his name's sake. Even though I walk through the valley of the shadow of death, I will fear no evil, for you are with me; your rod and your staff, they comfort me."

A crack forked through the television screen, distorting the image.

Esme shrieked and her fingers dug into Davis' arm.

On the wall, a print of a café in Paris swayed back and forth, then flew towards the priest.

Father Micheal ducked. The bottom of the frame grazed the side of his head. A line of blood trickled from the top of his ear. He righted himself then continued flicking holy water. "In the name of the Lord, evil spirit, I command thee to leave this house."

Esme's forehead shone with sweat. She covered her mouth but didn't scream.

Cold, ghostly fingers tickled the back of Davis' neck. He spun and glanced around the room, resisting the urge to run out the door and never return. Did Peter lash out because the prayers were working, or to show them the words had no effect? He followed the priest into the dining room, grateful Father Micheal hadn't cut and run.

"A human spirit isn't normally this strong. Evil is at play here." Father Micheal continued sprinkling holy water and forged ahead to the dining room. "Have you brought any evil objects into this house?"

"Um, no. Not that I'm aware of." Davis didn't want to let go of that book after wanting an original first edition of *The Turn of the Screw* for so long.

Esme studied him as if sensing his untruth.

Father Micheal spun with the cross held out in front of him. "Lord, we beg you to visit this house and banish from it all the deadly power of the enemy." He turned the corner into Davis' reading nook. "May your holy angels dwell here to keep us in peace, and may your blessings be upon us always. We ask this through Christ our Lord. Amen."

A loud and unearthly growl surrounded them.

Esme's eyes travelled the room.

Davis cringed as her gaze moved to his bookshelf.

She went to the shelf and pulled *The Turn of the Screw* out. "You bought this at The Tome Boutique, didn't you? After I asked you to stay away from my father's books."

Lying wouldn't get him anywhere at this point. All she had to do was ask Mr. Conway and he'd tell her. "Yes."

She held the book out to Father Micheal. "I consigned this at that store. My father died with this book in his arms. It could be the evil object you asked about."

Father Micheal sprinkled the cover of the book with holy water, and the growls grew in intensity.

"Ouch. It's hot." Esme dropped the book, and it landed on the floor.

Davis wanted to cry as smoke rose from the surface of the dust jacket. His precious books floated off the shelves and flew towards them. Davis covered his face to ward off the blows as his favorite books pelted him.

Father Micheal picked up *The Turn of the Screw* by the corners, held it in front of him, and ran towards the living room. "We must burn this book!"

Pictures flew off the walls. The candlesticks and coasters from the top of the dining table levitated and soared around the house. The objects followed them from the dining room to the living room.

Davis asked, "Is there no other way? You can't bless it and cleanse the negative energy?"

Father Micheal threw the book in the fireplace. "It is an artifact of evil." He placed his cross on the smoking book jacket and the edges of the cream-colored pages flamed.

Esme tossed kindling on the cover. "I'm sorry. We don't have a choice."

Davis hung his head as the kindling caught and his book smoldered. He wanted to be rid of Peter McFadden, but books comforted him in a way nothing else did. The television remote smacked him in the arm, landed on the hardwood floor, and smashed into pieces. With the television destroyed, what did it matter?

As the book reduced to nothing, the wailing ceased, and the objects flying around the house dropped from the air. Books thudded on the table and the floor. The metal candlesticks from the dining room table clunked on the floor a foot away from him.

Father Micheal said, "Burning the book seems to have cast the evil from the house. I'll bless every room to be sure before I leave."

The lingering smoke in the air that hadn't vented tickled Davis' throat and he coughed. "Thank you, Father." He opened the living room window.

"Yes, thank you. Now that things have stopped flying, I'll show you the rest of the house." Esme led the priest to the hallway. "The bedrooms, the bathroom, and the living room are this way." She stopped to rehang a picture on the wall.

Davis pulled his coat on and stepped outside. If Peter had

truly left, then Ezekiel probably followed. He circled the Rocky Mountain juniper tree. A black feather rested on the dormant grass, but otherwise, there was no sign of Ezekiel.

He tucked the feather in his pocket, and his hands brushed Esme's car keys. With the ghost gone, he may as well bring their bags inside the house. He popped the trunk and slung his backpack and Esme's gym bag over his shoulder.

Davis set their bags down in a corner away from the broken glass pieces of his light fixture. The broken glass needed to be dealt with before someone got hurt. With the broom and the dustpan from the tall cabinet in the corner of the kitchen, he set about corralling pieces of glass.

He kneeled to sweep his pile of debris into the dustpan and the side of his foot collided with Esme's gym bag and it toppled over. Something hard clanged on the floor. A sense of dread overcame him, and he chalked it up to the terrifying episode he'd endured during the house cleaning.

He lifted the bag. A set of pliers rested on his hardwood floor, and a rusted brownish-red residue coated the metal. His legs wobbled and he leaned on the wall to stay upright as a memory overwhelmed him.

Esme, wearing her dark blue coat and a baseball cap, had run from the house across the street, then had disappeared around a corner.

In a detached sense, he knew it was Lucy's house Esme had run from, even though he'd never been there before. With no control over his actions, he crossed the street and went inside the house.

Lucy lay on the floor unmoving, with vacant, wide-open eyes. He crouched beside her and pulled her into his arms, cradling her as tears filled his eyes.

Davis snapped himself out of the memory, Peter's memory combined with his own.

I'm not a murderer! But the real killer is inside my house!

His ears rang. He yanked his phone out of his pocket and dialed 911.

Esme's voice neared. Her and Father Micheal came around the corner.

Shit! Davis froze, unsure what to do. If he touched the pliers, he'd get his fingerprints on them and he'd implicate himself.

He dropped Esme's gym bag on top of the pliers, then raised his gaze.

Esme's eyes were fixed on the floor.

Oh no! Did she see the pliers?

A voice came out of the speaker of his phone. "What's your emergency?"

Davis stood in place, clutching the broom in one hand and his phone in the other.

Esme frowned. "Oh, Davis. You shouldn't have done that." She spun and ran towards the kitchen.

Davis snapped himself out of it and put the phone to his ear. "Police! My girlfriend is a murderer and she's at my house." He gave them the address, then shoved the phone in his pocket. "Father, run! She's a murderer."

The priest tutted. "What nonsense."

The distinctive metallic swooshing of a knife leaving the block in his kitchen, pierced the air. Esme ran towards them with a butcher knife in her hand.

Davis dropped the broom and tugged on the priest's arm. "Come on!"

"No." Father Micheal held up his cross. "Saint Michael the Archangel, defend us battle! Be our protection against the wickedness and snares of the devil..."

Esme laughed. "It won't work, Father. I'm not possessed." She sunk the knife to the hilt inside Father Micheal's chest, then ripped it out. Blood arced in the air and splattered on the walls and the floor.

Father Micheal dropped his Bible and holy water and clutched the wound in his chest. He collapsed onto his knees.

Esme stepped around the priest and smiled at Davis. "It's your turn to die, lover." She closed the distance between them.

Davis' hands trembled violently as he fumbled with the doorknob. *Jesus Christ, help me open this door.*

He twisted the doorknob and stepped onto the front porch, then slammed the door into Esme's face, knocking her backwards, and ran. His legs had the stability of spaghetti noodles. He risked a glance over his shoulder. Blood poured from Esme's nose, but still she pursued him. Metal jangled in his pocket.

Esme's keys!

Davis reached in his pocket and touched the key fob. The locks on the door of her car raised. He yanked the door open, jumped inside, then pressed the lock button on the driver's door.

"Let me in." Esme pounded on the window beside his head.

"No! You murdered a priest, and you have a butcher knife in your hand."

"I love you. I won't hurt you. Nothing has to change. Let's get our bags and drive away from here. We can go anywhere you want and start over."

Sirens wailed.

Esme pounded on the window. "Please!"

Multiple squad cars raced to his house, blocking the driveway and the street. Police officers raced out and surrounded them with their service weapons aimed at Esme.

"Step away from the vehicle and drop the knife."

Esme's eyes filled with malice. "You betrayed me, Davis."

A police officer crept up behind Esme.

"Are you kidding me?" Davis kept the conversation going to keep Esme's attention on him. He lowered the window a crack. "You're a murderer! You killed your own sister."

"She was a cold-hearted bitch. She deserved it."

"Did you stop to think about your mother? With you in prison, she has no one."

"That's your fault," Esme spat. "If you had of kept your mouth shut, no one would've ever known."

The police officer grabbed Esme's wrist and squeezed. "Ma'am, you're being detained."

The knife slipped from her grip and the police officer slapped cuffs on her wrists, then shoved her in the back of his squad car.

Never once had she ever shown Davis that side of her personality. He never would've believed she could be a killer.

One of the detectives they'd met at Mary Engelbert's house approached Esme's car.

Davis climbed out and handed her keys to Detective Swanson. "We need an ambulance right away. She stabbed Father Micheal in the chest. He's inside my house."

Detective Swanson grabbed the nearest police officer by the arm. "Radio for an ambulance then administer first aid to the priest inside the house until they arrive." He turned to Davis. "Do you need medical assistance? Did she hurt you?"

"No. I told the priest to run after the bloody pliers fell out of her gym bag, but he wouldn't listen."

"Bloody pliers?"

"Yes, under her gym bag. I knocked into her bag accidentally and they fell out. Then she went ballistic and grabbed the kitchen knife. She confessed to killing her sister Lucy."

The detective shook his head. "Like father, like daughter. It's a good thing you stumbled on those pliers. With the clever alibi she set up for herself, we probably never would've caught her."

Caw!

Ezekiel landed on the top of the squad car Esme sat in. "Razzhole!" He lifted off the car, then flew toward Davis.

Davis froze as the rubbery sound of his wings drew closer.

Ezekiel landed on his shoulder. "Mazzter!"

Davis gazed into the crow's beady eyes. Up close, they didn't appear as menacing. Maybe Ezekiel had simply found himself with the wrong crowd and needed a friend. Davis never imagined owning a bird. A cat maybe. Since his girlfriend turned out to be a murderer, loneliness lay on the horizon.

"Okay, Ezekiel. I'll be your master. But we need to work on your potty mouth around company."

Acknowledgments

Any author can attest to the many hours, self-doubt, and mood swings that are a part of writing a book. It takes special people in our lives to keep us going. In my case, I have the best husband and kids (human and furry) in the world. Yes, I'm biased. I also have a wonderful and supportive extended family, friends, and the support of many wonderful social media friends, book reviewers, influencers, and readers. And I have also been blessed to find two publishing houses with wonderful staff that took a chance on me.

I'm extremely thankful for all of them

About the Author

Michelle Godard-Richer is a multi-award-winning thriller and horror author with an Honours Degree in Criminology from the University of Ottawa. She was named Best Canada Author of the Year by N.N. Light's Book Heaven and earned a Crowned Heart from Ind'Tale Magazine.

Her fascination with crime and human behavior, combined with a lifelong passion for the written word, led her to realize a childhood dream of becoming an author. She enjoys crafting strong protagonists and diabolical villains with realistic and believable characteristics while making their lives as complicated and dangerous as possible.

When she isn't writing, you'll find her in the garden or with her nose in a book. She lives in the foothills of the Rocky Mountains in Alberta with her husband, two children, four dogs, and a cat.

To learn more about Michelle Godard-Richer and discover more Next Chapter authors, visit our website at www.nextchapter.pub.

Spine Chilling
ISBN: 978-4-82419-760-3

Published by
Next Chapter
2-5-6 SANNO
SANNO BRIDGE
143-0023 Ota-Ku, Tokyo
+818035793528

5th September 2024

Milton Keynes UK
Ingram Content Group UK Ltd.
UKHW042307101024
449571UK00003B/29